SARAH BEAR & SWEET SIDNEY

NANCY PATZ

Four Winds Press   New York

To my father with love

To Roy —
with every
good wish!

Nancy
Patz

July 1, 2001

Four Winds Press, Macmillan Publishing Company, 866 Third Avenue, New York, NY 10022. Collier Macmillan Canada, Inc.
Printed and bound in Japan.   First American edition   10 9 8 7 6 5 4 3 2 1

The text of this book is set in 14 point Cartier. The illustrations are rendered in pencil, watercolor, and inks.

Patz, Nancy. Sarah Bear and Sweet Sidney / by Nancy Patz.—1st ed.   p.   cm.
Summary: Sweet Sidney wakes up and begins to prepare eagerly for spring's arrival,
but Sarah Bear insists it's still too dark and cold.
ISBN 0-02-770270-7
[1. Spring—Fiction. 2. Bears—Fiction.] I. Title. PZ7.P27833Sar   1989   [E]—dc19   88-21300   CIP   AC

Day after day the house in the woods was quiet, so quiet—and cold.

Suddenly Sweet Sidney hollered, "*Wake up*, Sarah Bear! It's practically spring!"
He shook the big bump beside him.

"We've got to get ready," Sweet Sidney said.

"It's much too dark!" said the bump in the bed.

"Well, I'll get started,"
Sweet Sidney called.
And he swooped up sweaters
and waterproof boots,
fuzzy old mittens
and woolly knit suits.
He plopped the clothes
in the Winter Box.

"Oh, there's my Sarah Bear's
favorite jacket. I'll fold it
and pack it on top!" he said.
He clicked the locks
on the Winter Box
and shoved it into the closet.

"And now it must be spring, I know!
Wake up, Sarah Bear!"

But deep, down deep, way under the covers, Sarah Bear sleepily, grumpily said,
"Not yet, Sweet Sidney—it's much too early."

"But the *daffodils* are blooming, I'm sure! Just look!"
Sweet Sidney yanked at the curtains....

"Oh, my!" he gasped. "Not yet!"
And he was so disappointed.

He tried this and that to pass the time. Then he got a fine idea.

"*Wake up*, Sarah Bear!" he shouted. "Let's shine up this house for spring!"

But Sarah Bear just burrowed deep.

"Aahh-pumpf! Zzz-lumpfitty-rumph!" she mumbled.

"Well, I'll get started," Sweet Sidney said.

"Good idea," said the bump in the bed.

Sweet Sidney hauled out
the big straw broom
and *whomped* his way
through the living room.
He punched all the pillows
and smoothed out the lace,
scooped up the embers,
and swept the fireplace.

"Ohh...dust off the teacups!
Shake out the mat!"
He jiggled it here....
He wiggled it there....
"Sarah Bear does it like *that!*" he said.

"Then pick-a-pack-of-papers up
and pile them into stacks!
Swish away the spiderwebs!
Poke in all the cracks!
And now I *know* it's spring," he said.
"*Wake up*, Sarah Bear!"

But deep, down deep, way under the covers, Sarah Bear shivered.
"Not yet, Sweet Sidney—it's much too cold."

"But the *robins* are singing, I'm sure! Just listen!"
Sweet Sidney pushed open the window....

"Not yet?" he exclaimed. "NOT YET?"
And he was *so* disappointed.

He plunked his cello to pass the time. Then he got a good idea.
"*Wake up*, Sarah Bear! Let's fix a spring picnic!"
But deep, down deep, way under the covers,
Sarah Bear just grumbled, "Aahh-ZZUMPF!"

"Well, I'll get started," Sweet Sidney said.
"Good idea," said the bump in the bed.

Sweet Sidney pulled out
the pans and the bowls
and the beater he needed
for honey-nut rolls.
"I'll beat up a batter
of tickleberry shoots
(one cup, chopped fine!)
and sassafras roots...
walnuts and peanuts
and sugarplum-tree nuts...
and crumbly bumblebee-honey!"

Sweet Sidney licked
the honey cup clean
and popped the rolls in the oven.

"I always can tell
by the honey-nut smell
when the rolls are
golden and ready!" he said.
"Now there! *Wake up*, Sarah Bear!

"It's certainly spring by *now!*"
He peeped outside the window....

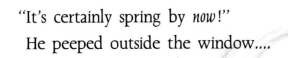

"Not yet! *Not yet!* NOT YET!" he roared, mad as a bear can get.

"Well, I'll just sit here and *wait!*" he said,
and he flopped himself down in his chair.

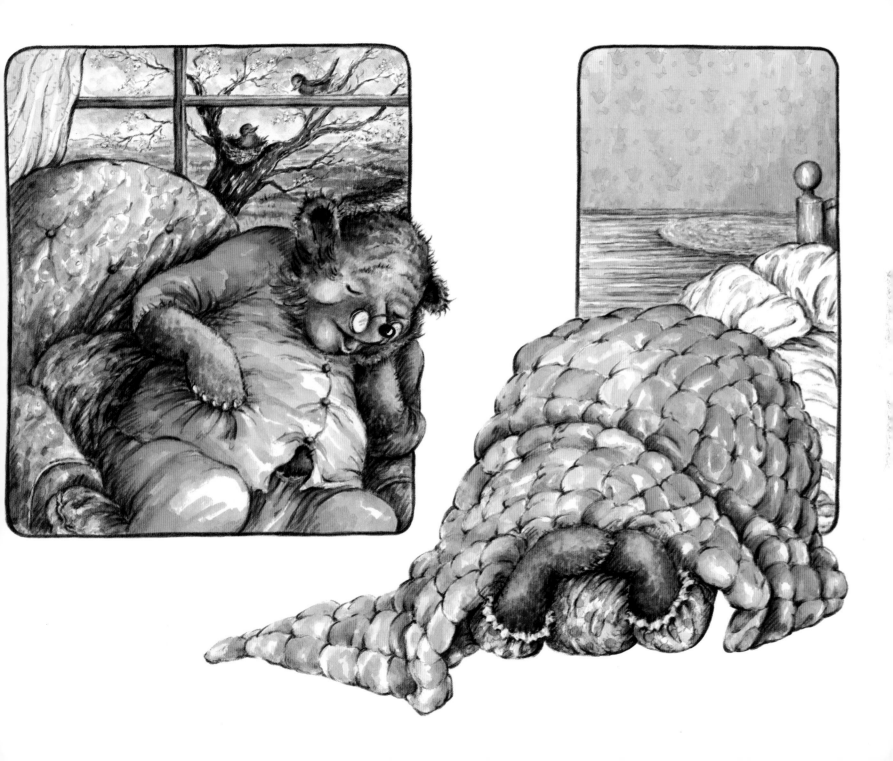

Sweet Sidney slept for days...

and days....

But Sarah Bear woke up!
"*Holy potatoes!*
He's sleeping through spring!
I'd better get busy!" she said.
Quietly, very quietly,
she tiptoed off to the kitchen...

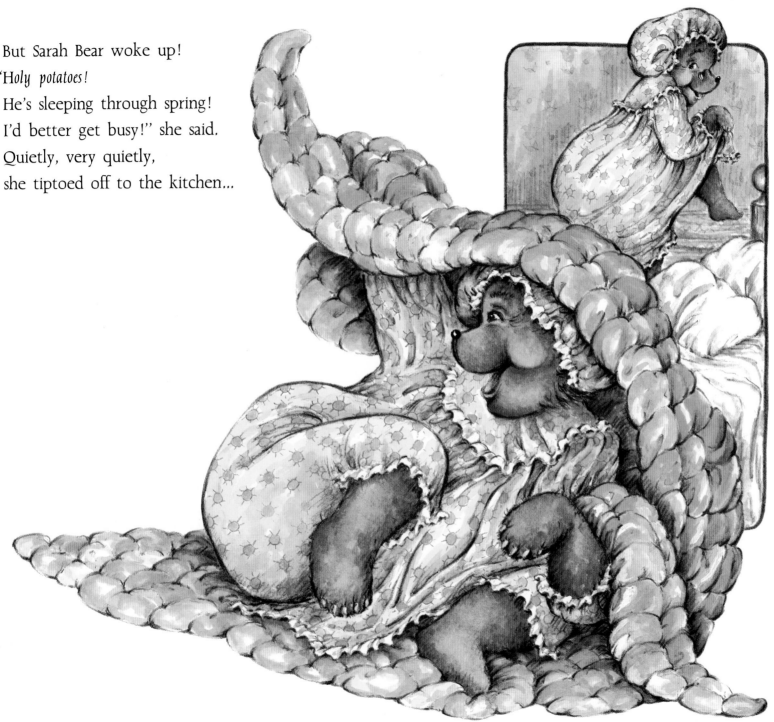

and sniffed her way
right to the picnic.
"*Yum!* What a scrumptious surprise!"
she cried. "No wonder
that sweetie's so tired!"

She mixed a big pitcher
of cranberry punch,
baked a fig pudding
and packed up the lunch.

Then she opened
the Springtime Box.
"Oh, here's Sweet Sidney's
favorite cap. He'll need it
right after his nap, I bet.
And *I* need a new spring bonnet!

With white apple blossoms!
And sugarplum-tree nuts!
Pink tickleberries!
Thick chains of peanuts!
And *miles* of wide ribbon
of daffodil yellow!

"Sweet Sidney will love it, I'm sure," she said,
"'cause this is a simply sensational hat!

And now I think I'm quite ready...."

Gently she whispered, "Ready for daffodils,
Sleepy Sweet Sidney? It's finally spring!"
"At last!" he shouted. "At *last, at last!*"

And off they pranced to the meadow....

"Oh, what a dilly of a daffodilly day!" Sweet Sidney roared,
loud as he could. And they laughed together in the breeze.

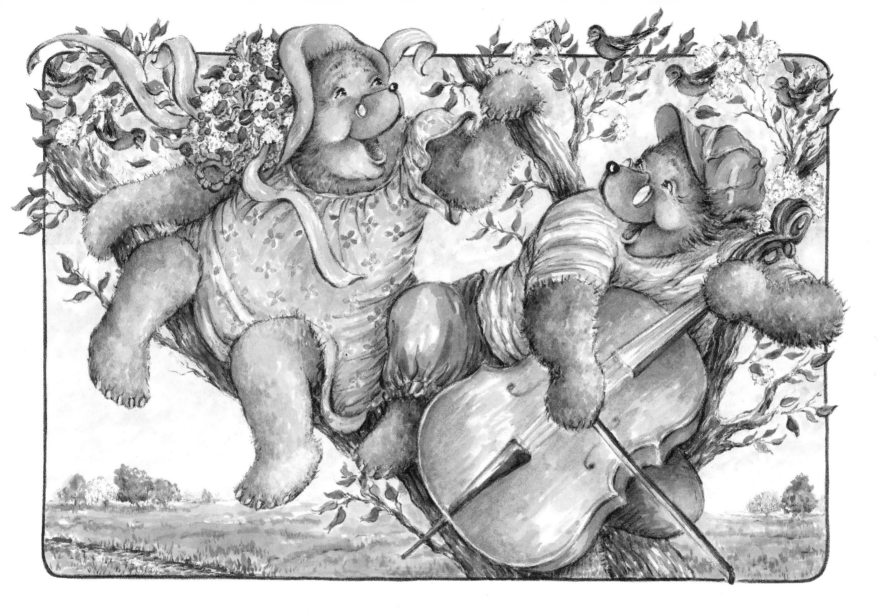

Day after day they sang with the robins
and watched the leaves grow greener....

And they walked by the stream picking tickleberry shoots
to chop up fine with the sassafras roots
they baked in the bumblebee honey-nut rolls
and ate with pudding at their picnics.

And they talked to each other in their favorite way:

"Sarah Bear, *you* are a daffodilly-dumplin'!"

"*You*, Sweet Thing, are a funny-bunny honey-bear!"

Oh, how they laughed in the sunshine...

day after springtime day.